The OMG Blog

Conkers

First published in 2016 in Great Britain by
Barrington Stoke Ltd
18 Walker Street, Edinburgh, EH3 7LP

www.barringtonstoke.co.uk

Text © 2016 Karen McCombie
Images © Shutterstock

A CIP catalogue record for this book is available
from the British Library upon request

ISBN: 978-1-78112-543-4

Printed and bound by CPI Group (UK) Ltd, Croydon, CR0 4YY

The OMG Blog

KAREN McCOMBIE

For Faith Jackson – the reluctant reader
who caught the book bug and is now unstoppable!

Contents

CONTENTS

CHAPTER 1

little Miss MESS-UP

Jessie had messed up.

She dreaded telling Mum. She wasn't *going* to tell Mum. Cos her big sister Clare never messed up. Clare was the perfect daughter and the perfect student. Little Miss Perfect.

Jessie often wished she was as perfect and clever as Clare. *And* brave. Don't forget brave.

If Clare ever messed up (fat chance), Jessie bet she'd be bold and brave and just face up to it.

Jessie was struggling to do that. Same as she was struggling to settle in at secondary school.

And right now she needed to be in the school library. But instead she was hovering in the corridor just outside, her heart thumping and full of dread.

"I'll just read this first," Jessie muttered to herself. Looking at the notice board would give her time to work up the nerve to go in. But it was hard to be interested in the stuff pinned on the board.

One A4 sheet had a message about homework club being cancelled this week. (Snore.)

One was a poster for a blog-site some Year 7 students had made. It was about rugby. (Double snore.)

One was a stern message from Mr Frazer, the Head Teacher, about the importance of wearing school uniform correctly. (A student had written 'Whatever!' on that.)

Jessie read each bit of paper three times. She was just going to read them for the *fourth* time when she felt a wibble-wobble in her blazer pocket. Someone was texting her.

OK, so it had to be Mum. Mum *always* texted about a minute after the school bell went at the end of the day. The text often came before Jessie was even out of the school gates. Jessie grabbed her mobile and read Mum's message.

> Hi, Jess-kin! I'm just finishing here. Shall we meet at the front office in five minutes and walk home together?

Jessie's heart sank.

Mum was always around school – but she wasn't a teacher or a member of staff. Her *real* job was doing accounts for small businesses. But she worked from home, and that gave Jessie's mum time to run the school Parents' Association.

That's why she was around so much, planning fund-raising events, like the quiz night, the summer fair and the festive bazaar.

Jessie had started at Newton Academy just two weeks ago but she was already fed up of bumping into Mum all the time. Her big sister Clare had warned her it would be like this. Clare had just moved away and into a student flat and had told Jessie that she couldn't wait to start at university. Mainly cos it would be bliss to walk to class without running into Mum.

Clare said she still cringed when she remembered the time Mum had stopped her on the way to PE and insisted on fixing her tie – in front of all Clare's friends *and* a boy she really liked.

Jessie texted Mum back.

> I'm not leaving yet. I'm going to Homework Club with a friend.

Jessie bit her lip and pressed 'send'. She hated lying to Mum.

Here's the truth. She wasn't going to Homework Club.

Here's *another* truth. She wasn't with a friend – she hadn't made any of those so far.

All the girls in her form class were friends with people from their old primary schools. And the only girls at Newton Academy from Jessie's old primary school were already in a little gang of their own. Which didn't include Jessie.

Oh, I didn't realise there was a Homework Club on a Monday! But glad to hear it and glad you're going. Text me when you're on your way back, my hard-working girl!

Jessie felt awful when she read her mum's text. Today she *hadn't* worked hard – in one lesson at least – and she was in trouble cos of it.

Little Miss Mess-Up.

Oh boy, Mum would be *so* disappointed with her if she knew! And Mum always wanted to know *everything* that was going on with Jessie and Clare.

Jessie frowned as she pinged Mum a smiley face emoji.

Then she pinged off a frantic WhatsApp message to her sister.

Clare
Online

Hey sis – school sucks. I have no friends. Mum is driving me mad. (She still thinks I'll turn into a mini-you. Ha!) Call me tonight? J x

15:36 ✓✓

With that done, Jessie switched the phone to silent, put it back in her pocket and took a deep breath.

"Here goes," she muttered, as she pushed the library door open ...

CHAPTER 2

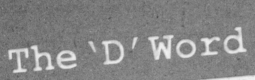

The 'D' Word

The library door made a loud screeching sound.

Everyone glanced up from the tables scattered around the big room. Boys and girls, older and younger, all looking fed up and gloomy. And all of them – like Jessie – here for the same reason. The 'D' word.

She just wished they wouldn't stare. Her cheeks were burning hot with embarrassment.

"Hello!" said a chirpy voice.

Jessie turned to see the friendly face of her ICT teacher, Miss Singh. So *she* was the teacher on duty today. That made the stress sink from Jessie's shoulders a little. Some of the teachers at Newton Academy were a bit stern and scary, but Miss Singh wasn't like that. She was young-ish

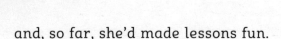

and, so far, she'd made lessons fun.

"Can I help you, Jessie?" Miss Singh asked with a warm smile.

Jessie gulped.

"I'm here, um, for, um ..." Jessie struggled with the words. "... for Detention."

"Oh! Really?" said Miss Singh, her perfect dark eyebrows raised in surprise.

Jessie understood why her teacher was surprised. So far, she'd always been such a good student (even if she wasn't as smart as her sister). Being a good student was what Mum expected of Jessie. And Mum said the teachers here at Newton Academy would expect it too, just cos she was Clare's sister.

Which meant that whatever she did, Jessie always felt she was letting someone down.

"Well, you'd better sit over there, with some other girls in your year group," said Miss Singh, her voice and smile not so warm any more. She pointed to a table by the window, and then scribbled something in a register.

Jessie walked slowly over to the table. She was glad to see that almost everyone had lost interest in her by now, and had their heads bent down over their books again.

OK, so *almost* everyone had lost interest in her.

Two girls were watching as she came closer to their table. One was wearing a navy headscarf, and one had a face so pale and eyes so wide that she looked a bit like a worried ghost.

A third girl was slouched over the table with her head on her arms, a mass of tight, dark curls fanned out over her shoulders.

Jessie had seen the girl with the headscarf before. She'd stood behind her in lunch queue one day and admired the twinkly glass pin that held the scarf in place.

"Hi," whispered the girl in the headscarf, lifting her backpack off the one spare seat so Jessie could sit down.

"Hi," muttered Jessie, slipping into the seat as silently as she could. (She didn't want to risk any more screeches or stares.)

"I'm Zarah, and this is Rose," said the girl, pointing to the pale, worried-looking student. "And *she's* Shanice."

Jessie glanced at Shanice, though all she could see of her was the top of her curly head.

Shanice didn't look up – she just raised a

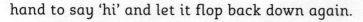

hand to say 'hi' and let it flop back down again.

"I'm Jessie. Do you, er, all know each other already?"

"We've seen each other around," said Zarah, "but we've only just properly met each other here, now. At the social whirl that is Detention."

Jessie nodded as Zarah spoke. At the same time, she stared at the girl called Shanice, who was still slouched over the table. Jessie wondered if she was OK. Zarah noticed her looking.

"Shanice says her mum's going to kill her for being in Detention," Zarah explained in a super-soft voice, so Miss Singh didn't hear.

That got Shanice's head flipping up, making her halo of hair bounce.

"It's no joke!" said Shanice, though no one was joking or sniggering. "My mum is going to do her loudest foghorn on me tonight. She'll yell at me for hours, I bet. I tell you, I need to buy super-strength earplugs on the way home!"

Jessie was too shy to ask what Shanice had done to deserve Detention, but Zarah jumped in and told her anyway.

"She rolled her skirt up *really* short."

"How harsh is that?" said Shanice. "I mean, I got 90% in my science test this morning. I just got moved to top set for maths. And I get a hard time cos my skirt is too short? Ha!"

Well, Shanice's mum might be loud, Jessie thought, *but Shanice is sounding pretty foghorn-ish herself*. And that didn't seem a great idea in a quiet library.

"Shh!" Zarah shushed Shanice. "The thing is, school's gone really strict on uniform this year.

My big brother Kamran is in Sixth Form and he says it didn't used to be so bad."

Jessie still felt rumbles of shyness and guilt in her chest, but Zarah's chattiness was starting to make her relax.

"My sister told me that too," whispered Jessie. "But she doesn't go here any more. She's at university."

"Hey, speaking of school being strict," said Zarah, "check this out …"

She gave a quick glance round and then pulled her headscarf back just a little – and Jessie and the girls got a sneak peek of something surprising.

A bright red streak in Zarah's dark brown hair.

"My big cousin Maryam did it," Zarah said

with a grin. "My mama is *so* mad with her – and me. But it's lucky I wear a scarf, or I'd get into trouble at school for sure!"

"So why did *you* get Detention?" Jessie asked, as Zarah deftly tidied her scarf again.

Zarah rolled her dark eyes. "My History teacher saw me looking at Instagram in class. But I was deleting a comment. It was *well* embarrassing. I mean, I couldn't let it stay on there!"

"What was the comment?" Rose whispered, joining in the chat for the first time.

"You mean *who* was it," Zarah replied. "At break-time I checked to see if anyone had commented on my photo of this cat in a glittery unicorn hat. And underneath someone had written, *SOOOO CUTE!!!*"

"So?" said Shanice, with a 'whatever' shrug.

Zarah rolled her long-lashed eyes before she replied. "It was my MAMA."

"No way! Your *mum*? Oh, that *is* bad," said Shanice, wrinkling her nose. "No wonder you had to delete that. It was totally worth the Detention!"

"Don't know about that," Zarah said with a fed-up sort of sigh.

That made Jessie think it might be Zarah's first ever Detention too. She had a funny feeling it wasn't Shanice's. And what about worried little Rose?

Zarah must have been thinking the same thing. "Hey, Rose, how come *you're* here?"

Rose's thin face flushed pink at Zarah's question.

"I told my French teacher that my dog ate

my homework," she replied, biting her lip. "He didn't think it was true."

"To be fair, it does sound like a pretty lame excuse," said Zarah.

"A big fat lie, you mean," muttered Shanice, waggling her finger at Rose.

"But my dog Rufus really *did* eat my homework!" Rose insisted. "My Mum Kim left her toast on top of my workbook and Rufus chewed them both ..."

Giggling was the last thing Jessie had expected to do during Detention. But here she was, slapping her hands over her mouth so Miss Singh didn't catch her.

"And what about *you*?" Zarah whispered to Jessie.

"I got told off in Maths for not listening,"

said Jessie, suddenly feeling bad again. "But I didn't hear the teacher cos –"

SLAP!

Jessie and the other girls jumped as Miss Singh's hand landed sharply on the table.

Uh-oh.

Jessie was in trouble for the second time today. And it was *all* Mum's fault.

Jessie's Diary

Monday 19th September

Clare phoned home this evening.

As soon as Mum went out of the room I told Clare about getting Detention. I explained it was cos my Maths teacher saw me staring out the window when he was talking. I didn't even hear when he called my name. <u>All three times</u> he called it!

But I'd been watching Mum out in the playground. She was talking to my Form Teacher, and I bet you anything she was talking about ME.

That made Clare groan – Mum was always talking to or emailing her Form Teacher, wanting to

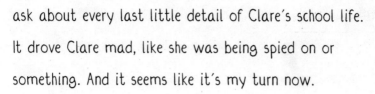

ask about every last little detail of Clare's school life. It drove Clare mad, like she was being spied on or something. And it seems like it's my turn now.

HELP!

The thing is, Clare doesn't understand that it's going to be MUCH worse for me. Cos Mum's going to push me hard to do as well as Clare and that's never going to happen.

Anyway, then I told Clare about Zarah and Rose and Shanice, and how Miss Singh came over to the four of us in the library. I'd thought Miss Singh was going to tell us off for chatting. Instead she gave us a form for a competition — one the ICT department are running. They want Year 7 students to work in groups, to develop blog-sites. The most popular one will win a prize! (The boring rugby blog I saw on the notice board this morning — that's an entry in the competition.)

Miss Singh challenged me, Zarah, Rose and Shanice to enter together. It was kind of exciting, but how can we start up a blog when we don't even know each other?

Clare said she's having to get to know other students fast at uni. She said you just have to be brave and talk to people and find out things that you have in common.

Brave ... that word again.

OK, I'm going to give it a go. I'm going to be brave. Tomorrow I'm going to get together with Zarah, Rose and Shanice and see what we have in common to blog about.

But I worry that we're all pretty different. I mean, Zarah is a chatterbox, Rose seems very nervy, Shanice is super-smart and scared of no one and I'm ... well, I'm kind of shy (and dumb – don't forget the dumb).

What if we don't have ANYTHING in common – except getting stuck in Detention today?

CHAPTER 3

Parent Problems

Jessie was ready to scribble down ideas for a new blog-site.

But so far this Tuesday lunchtime, all the four girls had done was moan about their mothers.

"Get this," said Shanice, slamming her pasta pot down on the picnic bench in the playground. "Mum was shouting at me for getting Detention WHEN WE WERE IN THE LIFT WITH OTHER PEOPLE!"

"Oh, shame!" murmured Rose, looking horrified.

"In front of your neighbours?" said Zarah, pulling a face.

"It gets worse," said Shanice, waving a plastic fork in the air. "*Then* she starts on about school being stupid, for ignoring my great marks and hassling me about my skirt being too short. And of course EVERYONE in the lift starts staring at my legs."

The other girls groaned in sympathy.

"*Then* Mum says she's going to come in and have a word with the Head Teacher today," Shanice carried on. "Says she wants to wave my SATs results in his face, to show him what really matters. I told her no *way* is she doing that. I don't want to bump into her – not if she's yelling her head off at Mr Frazer!"

"I worry about bumping into my mum at school all the time," said Jessie.

"But there's nothing wrong with *your* uniform!" Zarah joked.

"It's not that." Jessie sighed. "The thing is,

my mum's in charge of organising the Welcome Evening for Year 7 parents next week and she's in and out of here every five minutes. It's like having a stalker."

"Yeah, but what does she look like?" Shanice demanded to know.

Huh? Jessie felt confused. What did *that* matter?

"She, um, has brown hair like mine but a bit shorter," Jessie told Shanice. "And she mostly wears jeans and stripy T-shirts."

"So your mum looks like she works here, I bet," said Shanice.

"I suppose so ..." Jessie said with a shrug.

"She doesn't look like THIS, then ...?"

Shanice held up her phone and Jessie, Zarah and Rose leaned in to see the photo on the screen.

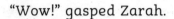

"Wow!" gasped Zarah.

Shanice's mum certainly was 'wow'.

The photo was taken in a normal coffee shop. Packed shopping bags sat by Shanice's mum's feet. But Shanice's mum looked more like she was dressed to go clubbing than to the supermarket. Her halterneck dress had a bold pattern of giant peacock feathers. Her short afro hair was dyed blonde. Her gold earrings were as big as plates. Her smile dared anyone to make a comment.

Now Jessie understood. Jessie stressed about her mum being in school – but the fact was, no one else would notice her.

But Shanice's mum turning up ... that would be like a one-woman party arriving in the drab school office.

"You get me?" said Shanice, clicking the

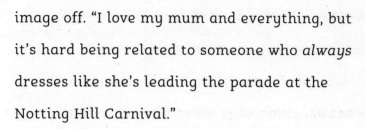

image off. "I love my mum and everything, but it's hard being related to someone who *always* dresses like she's leading the parade at the Notting Hill Carnival."

"My Mum Kim is a bit different too," Rose said in her soft voice. "Here ..."

While Rose rummaged in her bag, Jessie felt the familiar wibble-wobble in her blazer pocket. She sighed, ready for it to be Mum. But when she checked the caller ID, it wasn't Mum after all. Jessie sighed again anyway, cos it was her step-mum Tanya.

"Tanya-who-tries-too-hard" is what Clare always called her.

Tanya, who tried too hard to be Dad's 'best' wife, all kissy and huggy with him in front of Jessie and Clare. (Yuck!)

Tanya, who tried too hard to show Jessie and Clare what a fabulous step-mum she was, by being all gushy and 'thoughtful', always buying them stuff they didn't want. (Thanks, but no thanks.)

Tanya, who always referred to the girls' father as 'Daddy', even though they'd never called him that in their lives ...

Without being mean, it kind of made Jessie and Clare cringe to be around Tanya sometimes.

Jessie glanced back down at her phone.

> Hey, darling girl! Me and Daddy are SO looking forward to seeing you on Saturday. Just can't wait! Shall I make you your favourite tea? Love you lots, Tanya xx

"Wait! What *is* this?" she heard Shanice say. "I thought you were going to show us a photo of your mum, Rose."

When Jessie glanced up, she saw Shanice and Zarah frowning at a dog-eared postcard in Rose's hand. It was the sort that businesses put through your letterbox. The picture on the front certainly didn't look much like Rose. In fact, it didn't look much like a *woman* ...

CHAPTER 4

Twinkle Twinkle
little Stuff

Jessie, Zarah and Shanice had expected to see a woman who could be Rose's mum on the postcard.

Instead, they were staring at a photo of a *bicycle*.

"Mum Kim doesn't drive," said Rose. "This is how she gets around."

The bike was an old-fashioned one, painted white, with garlands of fake flowers tangled around the handlebars. It had a brown leather saddle and a wicker basket on the front with a sign that said, *Get Crafty!*

"Hey, I've seen your mum going around on that," said Shanice.

Jessie had too, and she'd seen the name *Get Crafty!* before, above a shop and café in town.

"Your mum runs that place?" said Jessie.

Rose frowned a little but nodded yes.

"It's cute," Jessie carried on. "I had my ninth birthday party there."

She remembered that party because it was the first one Dad had taken Tanya along to. Jessie had spent the party feeling a bit sick cos she ate lots of the chocolate hedgehog cake Mum had made for her AND tons of the pink and gold princess cake that Tanya had made specially for her.

But, apart from the excess of cake and Mum and Tanya pretending to be super-nice to each other, what Jessie remembered most was the party organiser. She must've been Rose's mum. She was tall with striking blue eyes. Her hair was up in a messy bun and she wore a long apron covered in paint. Soon all Jessie's friends were having a ball decorating T-shirts with felt and feathers and buttons.

"My Mum Kim runs art and pottery classes there," Rose explained. "Me and my family have the flat upstairs."

"Ooh, jealous! I love making stuff. See?" Zarah said, holding up her wrist to show off a beaded friendship bracelet.

"Sounds like a fun place to live," said Jessie.

"Don't know about fun, exactly," Rose replied, crinkling her nose. "Stuff for the shop ends up stacked in heaps in our flat. *Tons* of it."

"So?" said Shanice in her usual blunt way. "Paper, paint, glitter – that's all ... *twinkly* stuff. *Twinkly* mess. Try having a little brother who leaves smelly socks around. Or finding your mum's sweaty gym gear dumped over the radiators to 'air'. To stink the flat out more like."

"Yes, but my Mum Kim leaves half-finished craft projects everywhere," Rose explained. "She's obsessed with making collages out of old bits of broken china and random junk. And I really, really can't *stand* mess ..."

As Rose trailed off, Jessie spotted that she was nervously picking at her nails. Jessie really wanted to know more of Rose's story. Like why she called her mother 'Mum Kim', for instance. Did she call her father 'Dad Dave' or something? She was just about to ask when Zarah let out a loud groan and sunk her head into her hands.

"No! She's done it *again!*"

Zarah's phone was lying face up on the table, and she was frowning at an image on the screen.

"Who's done *what*?" asked Shanice.

"*This*," Zarah replied, spinning the phone around so the others could see it.

It was an Instagram selfie that Zarah had taken of all four girls when they first sat down to lunch. It had one comment by someone calling themselves 'mama2z'.

mama2z Loving you and your BFFs!!

"What IS my mama's problem?" moaned Zarah. "I *get* that she only lets Kamran on his sites and me on Instagram if she can see what we're doing. But why does she have to act like she's my best buddy too? And she gets it wrong all the time and says stupid stuff. Like now. I mean, it's not as if we're BFFs. We don't even *know* each other properly."

"True," said Shanice. "But it's worse than that. We don't know each other properly, *and* we don't have a single idea for a blog-site. *And* the closing date for the competition is next Monday."

The girls went silent. One minute they'd been chatting like old buddies, but now they felt awkward around each other. They were all feeling like the strangers they were.

Till Jessie realised something. Something important.

It was the something that all four of them had in common.

"Listen," Jessie said, excited by her new idea, letting go of her shyness. "Our mums – they make us feel all ... *grrrr*, right? And *that's* what we can blog about."

The three girls looked at Jessie and she felt a nasty lurch of fear – fear that she had overstepped the mark, fear that they might think *she* was laughing at their mums, fear that she had messed everything up, again.

But what Shanice did next sent Jessie's fear packing.

"Yeah!" she whooped. "That is one genius idea." She twirled her plastic fork in the air like a cheerleader's baton and caught it again.

"I love it!" said Zarah.

Rose just smiled and hugged herself with excitement.

Jessie beamed. She hadn't been able to breathe for a second there, but now she was thrilled that the other girls were so keen on her idea.

"Now we just need a name," Zarah pointed out. "I know – how about we call it ... *4 Cool Girls, 4 Crazy Mums*."

Zarah held up her hands for high-fives, and Jessie and Shanice were happy to slap them. The name was perfect.

But did Rose think so? She hadn't joined in with the high-fives, but then there weren't enough hands. Still, she didn't look totally happy.

"Have you got another idea, Rose?" Jessie checked with her.

She had just realised the *4 Cool Girls, 4 Crazy Mums* name wouldn't work anyway. Not if you included her step-mum Tanya. *4 Cool Girls, 4-and-a-half Crazy Mums* was too much of a mouthful.

"I ... I kind of like what you said, Jessie," Rose

replied. "About our mums making us *grrrr*! So it could be 'OMG'. Short for 'Our Mums – Grrrr'."

"OMG. Wow, *yes*, Rose," said Zarah.

"Well, it was really Jessie's –"

"Yeah, whatever, Rose," Shanice interrupted cheerfully. "Now all we need to decide is who blogs first. Bagsy me!"

Jessie was pleased to see Rose smile at Shanice's cheekiness. She'd been worried that Rose might be feeling hurt in some way.

"Not fair, ME!" said Zarah.

"No, me!" Rose joined in, her nerves vanishing in the excitement of the moment.

"ME! ME! I will!" Jessie laughed.

As the girls chattered and giggled, Jessie wondered if they were at the beginning of something.

The beginning of not being strangers any more.

Of being future BFFs maybe, fingers crossed ...?

OMG! ♡ ♡ ♡ ♡ ♡ ♡ ♡

Welcome to *Our Mums – Grrrr!* The blog where we tell our mothers we love THEM, but not the mad, bad and sad stuff they do!

→ ## THE PUSHY MUM ←

Posted by Jellybean

I am very proud to be the first blogger on this site. And I am very proud of my mum, who kept smiling and kept busy after our dad left five years ago.

But I'm also pleased to have a place where I can shout ...

MY MUM DRIVES ME CRAZY!

I swear she'd walk me to and from school every day if I let her (I don't).

I swear she'd email every one of my teachers each and every day to ask how I'm doing (if the school website had that info, which it doesn't).

I swear she'd sew a tracking device into my school blazer (*and* my out-of-school parka), if that was legal, which I don't think it is.

Hasn't my mother noticed that I'm in secondary school now and not five years old? Yes, I'm a bit shy. But I can still manage on my own. At least, I want to try.

I'd also like my mother to realise that I am not my big sister. And no matter how much you'd like it to be true, Mum, I will never be as smart and funny and brilliant as she is. I am your dumber daughter – get used to it.

So please, please, Mum – stop being so pushy.

I love you, but grrrrrrr!!

Jellybean

Posted Wednesday 21st September

CHAPTER 5

Really, really real

The living room door creaked open, just as Jessie finished typing her blog.

"Get out, Ty!" Shanice roared.

Jessie, Zarah and Rose all jumped.

But not Shanice's little brother, Ty. He just stood in the living room doorway and didn't even flinch at his sister's roaring. Jessie supposed that Shanice's family didn't notice the volume in the same way that she and the other girls did.

"Mum said to give you this," he mumbled, walking in with a tray of drinks and cookies. Jessie could see that the reason Ty was mumbling was because his mouth was crammed with half a chocolate chip cookie.

"Oh," said Shanice, softening, her voice at

a more normal volume. "OK. Put the tray on the table and THEN get out."

Since Shanice lived closest, the girls had piled back to her flat after school on Wednesday. They weren't just talking about the OMG! blog now – they were developing it. It had taken a while to choose the right template, but at last they'd stumbled on one that made them all go "yes!" at the same time.

Which was just as well. Zarah had heard that lots of students were entering the ICT competition. And with the closing date of Monday fast approaching, they had no time to waste.

"What are you doing?" asked Ty.

He put the tray down, took another cookie and tried to peek over the girls' shoulders at the computer screen.

When they'd first arrived back, Shanice had explained to her mum that she and the girls were working on a project for school and were *not* to be disturbed.

Her mum – who told the others to call her Joy – was fine about that. Which was just as well, too, considering what the blog was about. The last thing they needed was Ty telling her now.

"It's boring. It's homework. GO!" Shanice shouted, waving Ty away as if he was an annoying wasp.

"It's not fair. It's supposed to be *my* computer time now. I wanted to play Friv," Ty moaned as he crunched on the cookie, sprinkling crumbs all over the floor.

"You have an Xbox in your room," said Shanice.

Ty shrugged his shoulders. "What does 'OMG' stand for? Is it rude?" he asked, standing on his tiptoes to see better.

Shanice got off the stool, turned Ty around by the shoulders and shoved him towards the living room door.

"I'll tell Mum you're not being nice to me," Ty yelled.

"Yeah, yeah … bye," said Shanice, slamming the door shut behind him. "Right, are you ready to publish your post, Jessie?"

"Uh-huh," said Jessie, and she pressed the key that made the first ever OMG! blog go live. At the same time, it popped up on the open screen on her phone.

OMG! was really, *really* real!

Thrilled, the other girls cheered and clapped.

Jessie gazed at the screen on her phone, then at the computer screen and back again. She grinned to herself. Just having that moan about Mum made her feel a bit more independent.

In fact, it made her more confident about not responding to Mum's latest text, asking her how she was getting on. It was the *fourth* text Mum had sent since school ended. Jessie had already been in touch to let Mum know she was doing her 'homework' at her friend's flat instead of at school, and that she'd be back by 5.30 p.m.

Her mum really didn't need to keep checking in, asking how it was all going. Mum needed to learn to trust Jessie. Even if Jessie hadn't owned up and told her about getting Detention on Monday.

Remembering that made Jessie prickle with

guilt all over again. Not being trusted made her feel rubbish, but keeping secrets from her mum made her feel even more rubbish.

All of a sudden, she just wanted to get away from the blog and her guilt for a few minutes.

"Um, can I use your loo?" she asked Shanice.

"Sure," said Shanice. "It's the third door on the left."

Jessie hurried out of the living room, and let the door close behind her. Six identical sky-blue doors lined the hot-pink hall.

Jessie suddenly felt a bit like Alice in Wonderland. Only this wasn't Wonderland – it was a flat on the 14th floor of a high-rise tower block.

Now, which door was the bathroom? With her mind in a kerfuffle she'd completely forgotten what Shanice had just told her.

"Here goes," Jessie muttered to herself, and put her hand on the closest metal doorknob.

But the first door she tried turned out to be the airing cupboard. Jessie turned and randomly chose another door.

"Oh, sorry!" she said. *This* room was covered in red and blue FC Barcelona posters, and Ty was sprawled on the bed. He looked up from his Xbox and waved at her with yet another chocolate chip cookie in his hand.

Jessie quickly backed out and tried a *third* door. But it didn't open onto the bathroom either. As she stood in the kitchen doorway, Jessie felt the wibble-wobble of a phone alert in her back pocket. The blog was on her screen – was the alert to let her know there were comments on it already?

Maybe.

But Jessie didn't check. She was too frozen with shock. Cos she was face to face with a shaking, shimmying bottom ...

CHAPTER 6

Dance?
NO THANKS!

The shaking, shimmying bottom belonged to Shanice's mum, Joy.

When the girls had arrived, Joy had been wearing a long, patterned top over black, leather-look jeggings. But she'd gone off and got changed – now she was in orange and black zigzag running shorts and a matching neon vest. Was this the gym kit that Shanice had been moaning about? Jessie supposed so, from the dancing going on, and the jiggling bottom.

The strange thing was, Joy was definitely dancing, but the kitchen was *totally* silent.

Jessie shook herself, and tried to back out without being noticed. She did not want to be caught staring.

Too late – at that exact second, Joy twirled around.

"Whoah!" she roared, then pulled off a pair of headphones. "Just doing my Zumba practice. See?"

Joy stepped towards an iPod dock and Jessie jumped as the thundering blast of blaring Latin music filled the room.

"Can't keep still to a rhythm like this, can you?" Joy bellowed above the music.

Jessie said nothing and stood *very* still.

But not for long. Joy reached for Jessie's hands and tugged her closer to her neon chest. She then began doing something wriggly and squiggly with her hips, pulsing them from one side to the other.

Jessie was alarmed. It looked like a type of

dance called salsa that she'd seen on TV. Maybe on *Strictly Come Dancing* or something. But Jessie was doing the *opposite* of Joy's salsa wriggling and squiggling and hip-shimmies. Her style of dancing was called the Shy Girl Shuffle.

"Come on – loosen up and give it a go, girl!" Joy ordered Jessie. "Watch and learn. You put one foot forward, then put it right back. Put one foot forward, then put it right back. Your turn!"

Joy sounded just like one of those bossy, over-keen instructors at a fitness class.

Jessie put a foot forward and back but still felt frozen with embarrassment. "I don't think I can do it," she mumbled.

She felt madly uncomfortable. In fact, she'd rather curl up and die than salsa around the kitchen with someone else's mum.

"Nonsense," Joy exclaimed above the music. "Course you can. Try! Feel the music, Rose!"

"I'm Jessie ..."

"Feel the music, Jessie! One foot forward, then put it right back. Put one foot forward, then –"

BANG! BANG! BANG! BANG!!

A new noise startled Jessie. It was coming from above.

"Oh, shut up," Joy yelled at the ceiling. "You're no FUN, Mr O'Sullivan!"

Jessie could sympathise with this Mr O'Sullivan. It seemed that he was another person who didn't 'feel the music' when it came to salsa at 5 p.m. on a Wednesday.

"MUM!"

Jessie looked over her shoulder and saw

Shanice in the doorway. She looked furious. But Jessie was glad to see her – *and* to be rescued.

Now it was Shanice's turn to yell. Shanice stomped over to the iPod and turned the music off. Next, she snatched Jessie's hands away from her mum's.

"Can't you behave like a normal mother?" she snapped at Joy. "Just sometimes …"

"A boring mother, you mean?" Joy replied, laughing at Shanice as if she'd told the funniest joke.

Shanice narrowed her eyes at her mum.

"Aw, come here, my grumpy sweet potato and have a little dance with your mum …" Joy said, moving towards Shanice with her hands held out.

"No way!" yelped Shanice. She shoved Jessie

out of the kitchen and slammed the door shut behind her.

From inside the kitchen, Joy roared with laughter and turned her Latin beat straight back on again.

"I tell you, she is mad," Shanice hissed, as she stormed back to the living room with Jessie following.

"Hey, there you are," said Zarah, turning to Jessie. "Look – plenty of people have commented on your post already."

"Really?" said Jessie, so pleased and surprised at this news that she forgot the horror of what just happened in the kitchen. The alert that had made her phone vibrate in her back pocket – it must have been to let her know about these comments.

But Jessie left her phone where it was and hurried over to the computer screen. Holding her breath, she scrolled down to see what was under the post she'd written.

Zarah was right – there they were.

Three shiny new comments!

3 Comments   More →

Comment by **ZeeBee** ...

Poor you! Your mum sounds like a nightmare!

Reply   3 minutes ago

Comment by **Petal** ...

> You tell her. She's WAY too pushy!

Reply   2 minutes ago

Comment by **IceGirl** ...

> Grrrrrrrrr! ☺

Reply   2 minutes ago

Jessie was properly excited. Until she
thought about the names that went with the
comments ... Earlier, when they were walking to
Shanice's, the girls had decided to invent cute
blogger names for themselves.

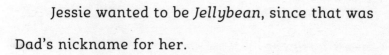

Jessie wanted to be *Jellybean*, since that was Dad's nickname for her.

Zarah had settled on *ZeeBee*. 'Zee' for Zarah, and 'Bee' for her last name, Bashir.

Rose wanted *Petal*, which was what her granny called her when she visited.

Shanice came up with *IceGirl*, just cos she said it sounded cool.

"OK, *I* get it," said Jessie, looking around at her friends.

Zarah and Rose were grinning at her, pleased with their tease. Shanice was not.

"Move over, Jessie," Shanice suddenly ordered her, waving Jessie away from the computer.

She moved. Fast.

Shanice's frown was pretty fierce.

Shanice plonked herself in the chair, stared

at the screen, then cracked her knuckles. She meant business.

"What are you going to do?" asked Rose, her voice wobbling.

"Well, Jessie got to blog first, cos OMG! was *her* idea," said Shanice, with her fingers already on the keyboard. "And I know we haven't decided whose turn it is next. But if I don't get to let off some steam about my mum now, I'll scream! The next blog-post is mine."

"Er, OK," said Rose.

She, Jessie and Zarah pulled faces at each other. But they understood.

Shanice really, *really* needed to do the next OMG! post, cos she was super-cross with her far too loud-and-proud mum.

And Jessie really, *really* needed the loo, she

remembered, and she hadn't found it yet.

"Be back in a minute," she said to her friends.

Jessie headed for the hall, keeping her fingers crossed that Joy wasn't still on the lookout for a shimmying salsa partner.

OMG! ♡ ♡ ♡ ♡ ♡ ♡ ♡

Welcome to *Our Mums - Grrrr!* The blog where
we tell our mothers we love THEM, but not the mad, bad and sad stuff they do!

→ THE EMBARRASSING MUM ←

Posted by IceGirl

My mum does not want to be boring, she says.

My mum does not want to be ordinary.

She says if life was on a dial, most people turn it to 4 or 5 out of 10.

My mum says, why stop at 10? Why not grab that dial and turn it up as high as you can, to 11!

Well, Mum, that might be a lot of fun for you.

BUT IT'S NOT A LOT OF FUN FOR ME!

I don't want you to be invisible. I don't want you to be all meek and boring. But can you sometimes – just *sometimes* – tone it down a bit?

Like at parents' evening ... do you have to dress in such a riot of colour that the teachers' eyes pop out of their heads?

Do you always have to talk LIKE YOU HAVE A MEGAPHONE, so everyone for miles around knows our business?

If I had one wish, it was that I could turn the 'EMBARRASSING MUM' dial down a couple of notches. Just down to a perfectly ordinary and unembarrassing 6 or 7. Just once in a while.

I love you, but grrrrrrr!!

Ice Girl

$\longrightarrow$

Posted Wednesday 21st September

CHAPTER 7

Time *for a* SHOUT-OUT

It was Thursday and the bell for break-time had just *brrrriiinnggg*ed.

Jessie was hurrying along the corridor, past the crush of students. She was on her way to the ICT room. Jessie and Zarah, Rose and Shanice had all had a note from Miss Singh asking them to come and meet her, and show her how they were getting on with their blog-site project.

Above the din of students' chat and laughter, Jessie heard her name being called. Or *nearly* her name.

"Hey, Jess-kin!"

She slowed down, knowing she had no choice but to say hello.

"Hi, Mum," said Jessie, squeezing a smile

onto her face. "Listen, can you *not* call me that at school?"

Jessie's mother pulled a jokey sad face.

"Sorry! I forgot. Your sister hated it if I called her 'Clare-Bear' around here."

I know, she told me, Jessie thought. And then, trying to get away, she said, "OK, Mum, I've got to go – my ICT teacher is expecting me."

"What's her name again? Miss Singh, isn't it?" Mum asked.

Of course Mum knew that. She'd memorised the names of all Jessie's teachers. She'd got a print-out of Jessie's timetable in her bag, as well as on the pin board in the kitchen. She knew better than Jessie what lessons she had and who her teachers were.

"Yes, it's Miss Singh. Look, I have to go and –"

"Do you have some homework to hand into her?" Mum interrupted. "I didn't see that in your online homework schedule when I checked it last night."

"No," Jessie replied, gritting her teeth. "Me and some friends –"

"Which friends?" Mum interrupted again. "Is one of them this Shanice? The one whose flat you went to yesterday?"

"Yes," Jessie sighed. "Anyway, Miss Singh wants me and Shanice and Zarah and Rose to ..."

Jessie flipped from feeling cross to guilty. She was about to fib to her mum again. She could hardly mention the blog, could she?

"... to come to her ICT club," Jessie said, squirming inside at her fib.

"Ooh, that sounds fun! When will that

happen? Which day?"

Jessie pretended not to hear. She started walking off, waving bye.

"Hold on!" Mum said, running after her. "Give these flyers to your friends, will you, Jess-kin? Whoops, sorry – Jessie. If they can hand them to their mums or dads that would be great. I need helpers to serve teas and coffees at the Welcome Evening next Monday."

Jessie grabbed the flyers and tried again to leave.

"See you at home later," Mum called after her. "And I saw you had some tricky maths homework. If you need a hand with that, you know numbers are my thing ..."

Mum's words got left behind in the crowd as Jessie sprinted down the corridor. She stuffed

Mum's stupid leaflets in her blazer pocket and ran up the stairs to the ICT room.

"Sorry I'm late," she gasped.

Miss Singh and Jessie's blog-buddies were already huddled around a computer.

"No worries," said Miss Singh. "I was just saying that the site's looking great, Jessie. I'm impressed by the design, as well as the idea. Well done to all of you!"

Jessie, Zarah, Rose and Shanice beamed with pride.

"And I like the fact that you're being positive too," said their teacher. "The way you finish your posts with '*I love you, but grrrrrr!!*' It's sweet and kind, so the blog is not just a big fat moan about mothers."

"Aw!" Shanice burst in. "*That's* what we

89

should have called it. *Big Fat Moan About Mothers!*"

Everyone laughed, even Miss Singh.

Still, Zarah reached over and put her hand across Shanice's mouth to keep her quiet. Shanice rolled her eyes and pretended to struggle.

"Anyway, we *wanted* it to be positive," said Zarah. "I love my mama – we *all* love our mums, even if they *do* drive us crazy."

"And when other students read the blog and make comments, they'll say they love their mums too. Hopefully!" said Jessie.

"OK ..." Miss Singh said slowly. "But other students – they are your problem now, aren't they?"

Jessie wondered what Miss Singh meant. So did the other girls – she could tell by their confused silence.

Miss Singh began to explain herself. She held her fingers up one by one as she made each point.

"This blog competition will be won by the group that has the best idea, the best design AND is the most popular blog with students here at Newton Academy."

Right, thought Jessie. So, Miss Singh had just said she really liked the OMG! design and idea. Only one thing was missing.

"We need lots of people to view our blog, don't we?" Jessie asked. "And respond to it ..."

"Today's Thursday. The competition closes on Monday," said Zarah. "So we need *lots* of views over the weekend."

"Exactly," Miss Singh said. "You need to think about how to let other students know the blog exists – and fast."

"We could make posters today," Jessie suggested.

"Yes, that's what two of the other groups have done," said Miss Singh, pointing to a couple of printed sheets on the ICT notice board. One of them was for the rugby blog Jessie had already seen.

"Wow. They look *well* boring," said Shanice. She'd shaken herself free of Zarah's hand, but maybe it should've stayed there.

Still, even if it *was* a bit rude of Shanice to say so, it was true. From where the girls were sitting, the two posters blended in with all the other flappy bits of paper pinned to the board.

"Well, we could set up an Instagram account to advertise the site," said Zarah, holding up her phone.

"Hmm. It might take you a while to get people to sign up that way," Miss Singh reminded them.

"I guess so," said Zarah, looking at her screen. "Still, lots of people at school *have* Instagram and – *NOOO!*"

Miss Singh looked alarmed – but Jessie, Rose and Shanice knew what was wrong.

"What? What's your mum written *this* time?" asked Shanice.

She grabbed Zarah's wrist and pulled her close to see the phone better. Jessie and Rose leaned forward too.

OK, so it seemed that Zarah had posted an old clip of Blondie singing the original, much cooler version of 'One Way or Another'. Fine. And, underneath, there were LOTS of comments.

The first was –

mama2z **Hey, that's got a great beat!**

which Jessie and her blog-buddies all knew
was Mrs Bashir.

Then Jessie began to read the comments
that followed – and felt *so* bad for Zarah. It was
awful to have your mum leave a corny comment
like that. But it was even WORSE when a whole
stack of people had written stuff like ...

bizzie_lizzie **Is that your mum?! Hahahaha!!**

ash_boy007 **Aw, Mummy likes your music ...
so sweet! NOT!**

"I am SO deleting my Instagram account," Zarah said, and began tip-tapping at her phone, her face a picture of pure frustration.

But suddenly Shanice grabbed Zarah's mobile from her and plonked the computer keyboard in front of her instead.

"Think it's *your* turn to blog, Zarah," she said with a grin. "Let all your *grrrr*s out!"

"Yes, write more posts, girls, but DO focus, too, on finding out how to get people reading them. The clock is tick-tick-ticking on the competition!" Miss Singh said.

But Jessie had already started to focus – on Rose. Miss Singh was right – it was time for a BIG shout-out for the blog. And quiet, anxious Rose was *just* the person to make that happen. Even if she didn't know it yet.

OMG! ♡ ♡ ♡ ♡ ♡ ♡ ♡

Welcome to *Our Mums - Grrrr!* The blog where we tell our mothers we love THEM, but not the mad, bad and sad stuff they do!

→ THE TOO-FRIENDLY MUM ←

Posted by ZeeBee

Lots of people I know argue with their mothers.

They argue about tidying their rooms.

They argue about who they hang out with.

They argue about wearing mascara to school. (Well, the girls do anyway. And one or two of the boys.)

And when I say argue, I mean *really* argue, ALL THE TIME.

I'd HATE to live like that.

I'd HATE for home to be all about shouting and

door-slamming and not liking each other very much.

So I'm pleased to say that I get on well with my mother.

I mean, yeah – I do stuff that makes her happy (my room is pretty tidy, and she never has to nag me about my homework, etc).

And she does nice stuff for me (she got me the mobile I wanted, she's the best cook, etc).

But here's what drives me crazy. She said I had to let her follow me if I joined Instagram. I said OK. Plenty of people's parents have that same rule.

The thing is, I bet other people's parents don't write EMBARRASSING comments on their posts!

Why does Mama want to act like my 'friend' on social media? Can't she just be normal and read my posts from time to time, to check I'm not online friends with an axe murderer or something?

Cos that's the point of parents peeking at your posts, isn't it? It's not to act like a 'mate', and make everyone at school think you're a total loser.

So, Mama, please be my mum and not my friend.

I love you, but grrrrrrr!!

ZeeBee

→

Posted Thursday 22nd September

CHAPTER 8

sparkles
AND SECRETS

The girls were mad about Jessie's idea.

Here's what she'd suggested – after school, they'd go back to Rose's. Her mum's craft shop was full of paint, glitter, sequins, feathers and sparkles, right? With all that, they'd be able to make posters for the blog that were a million times more silly, fun and eye-catching than anyone else's.

Tomorrow they'd get to school early and stick them up on every notice board. No one could miss them. Everyone would check out the blog.

Hopefully, stacks of people would post on the site over the weekend and – *shazam!* – the girls MIGHT just win the ICT blogging competition.

OK, so that wasn't totally the truth. Not *all* the girls were mad about Jessie's idea ...

When Jessie suggested it in the ICT room, Rose went whiter-than-white. It was as if she'd seen a ghost or been told her baby hamster had died or something.

But Zarah and Shanice whooped and yelled and said it was the best, most cool idea ever.

At last Rose had muttered, "All right then ..."

Zarah and Shanice were whooping too much to notice anything was wrong, but Jessie did. She felt bad – almost as if she'd bullied Rose into it.

Jessie *still* felt bad as the four of them walked towards the shop. Rose had hardly spoken a word on the way there. The look on her face was as if she was going to Detention again – possibly for the rest of her life – not taking her friends home for the first time.

"It looks busy," said Zarah, peeking in the

big glass window of *Get Crafty!*

"Mum Kim runs an after-school workshop for little kids on Thursdays," muttered Rose.

Jessie noticed Rose take a deep breath and gather herself before she pushed the door open.

What's that about? Jessie wondered.

She felt a bit worried. Was this going to be OK? Rose was always so quiet, mostly letting the others do the talking. They'd all spoken about their families, and had their Mum Moans, but Rose hadn't, not really.

In fact, it was Rose's turn to blog next, but now she thought about it, Jessie wasn't sure what exactly Rose would blog about. All she'd said was that her Mum Kim was a bit different. She'd also said that her Mum Kim was messy, and that she didn't like mess.

That didn't sound too awful. It wasn't as bad as having a pushy mum like Jessie's, or having a mum like Zarah's who stalked her online, or having a super-embarrassing, super-loud, salsa-loving, Zumba-practising mother like Shanice's.

Unless ...

Unless there was something Rose wasn't telling them.

"Hey, honey!" a tall woman called out to Rose as she pushed the door open.

Jessie recognised her from her long-ago birthday party. She looked exactly the same, with her piled-up messy bun and her paint-splattered apron.

And this was an after-school club and not a party, but the room had the same relaxed, fun vibe that Jessie remembered. All the kids were bent over long tables, drawing, doodling, giggling. Meanwhile, their parents were sitting at the back – in the café section of the shop – drinking coffee and chatting.

A woman with short dark hair was serving someone a big slab of carrot cake. Jessie's tummy rumbled – it looked so good. How amazing was it to live above a place like this? Where you could do art and eat carrot cake whenever you wanted to?

But Rose's face was set firmly in worry mode. She didn't seem to think *Get Crafty!* was an amazing place to call home at all.

"Hi," she mumbled to the woman who must be her Mum Kim. "These are my friends. Just going upstairs to do some homework ..."

With that, she headed to a nearby door with the others following behind.

"Hey," the waitress with the short dark hair called out before they disappeared. "Want some of my best carrot cake to take up with you?"

"No, thanks," said Rose, and she quickly waved the other girls up the stairs and shut the door behind them.

Jessie had no time to wish that Rose had said yes to that offer. She was too busy staring at all the stuff piled up on every step.

- Art books.

- Coloured paper.

- Soft mounds of felt.

- Jars of buttons and beads.

- Egg boxes and kitchen roll tubes that were waiting to be turned into works of art.

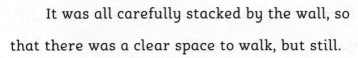

It was all carefully stacked by the wall, so that there was a clear space to walk, but still.

The flat wasn't exactly messy, but it was certainly cluttered and chaotic – just like Rose had warned them it would be.

WOOF! WOOF!! WOOF!!!

"Oh, no – someone forgot to close the stair-gate," Rose called out. "Stay, Rufus, stay!"

It was too late.

Claws clattered on the wooden steps. A blur of white and black fur hurtled down the stairs towards the girls.

Rufus's tail was wagging so much that it whacked against a mound of coloured tissue paper, which whirled down the stairs like confetti.

"You daft pup!" Rose said, smiling for the

first time. She grabbed the dog's collar and dragged him back upstairs.

Her friends followed, and found themselves in a big kitchen that looked more like the art department at school. There was normal kitchen stuff like a sink and a fridge and a cooker and table. But every wall was plastered with amazing artworks made of vintage bits of broken china and other found objects. It was like junk modelling for grown-ups. And every surface was cluttered with more jars and paints and craft bits and bobs.

"Where will we put this stuff?" asked Zarah. Like Jessie and Shanice she had a handful of tissue paper that she'd grabbed as it fluttered on the stairs.

"Put it anywhere," Rose said with a shrug. "It won't matter. Do you want to come up to my room for a second, before we make our posters?"

The girls – and Rufus the dog – all trooped up another set of stairs.

In this upside-down home, Jessie spotted the living room on this top floor (just as bright, colourful and random as the kitchen). There were two more doors – one covered with a montage of postcards of famous paintings, and one totally plain.

Rose opened the second door.

Rufus bounded into Rose's room first, and leaped up on the bed, curling himself up on a crisp, white duvet.

Jessie gazed around in surprise. She was trying not to gawp at how different this room was from the rest of the flat. The walls were white, the smooth floorboards were stained white, the furniture was white. There were no pictures on the walls, just a plain round mirror surrounded by snowflake fairy-lights. Some shelves held books and a few photos in clear glass frames. The only colour came from the glossy dark green leaves of a rubber plant by the window.

"Where is your stuff, Rose?" gasped Shanice. "Do you just shove it in your cupboards and drawers?"

"I put it away, if that's what you mean," said Rose. She shrugged off her blazer and tie, opened a wardrobe door, and hung her things up neatly.

"I thought MY room was tidy," said Zarah. "But this is amazing!"

"Wow. Your mum must *really* love you," Shanice carried on. "You're like a dream daughter ..."

"Don't know about that," replied Rose, her voice edged with sharpness. She bent down and took off her shoes, placing them on a rack at the bottom of the wardrobe.

Jessie watched her, wondering once again what Rose's story was. She moved closer to the shelves. Perhaps the framed photos could give her clues about Rose and her family.

"Your mum doesn't like your style, then?" asked Shanice.

"She keeps telling me I should be more creative with my room," said Rose. "But I am creative with it. It's just that her style's not *my* style. In fact, as far as my mum's concerned, Rufus is more artistic than me."

"You're musical, though," said Zarah.

Jessie turned at a sudden parpy *toot*.

Zarah was holding a clarinet and trying (and failing) to play it.

"Nope, I'm not musical either," said Rose, snatching the instrument from Zarah and putting it back on a stand that Jessie hadn't noticed before. "My parents make me do lessons, even though I'm rubbish."

"Why do they do that?" asked Zarah.

"They keep hoping I'll like what *they* like. See life the way they see it," said Rose. "Sometimes I think they don't get me at all ..."

"So that's what you can blog about," said Shanice. "It's your turn next, after all. You can write your first blog-post after we've made the posters."

"Um, I dunno ... I don't know if I want to." Rose had pink spots on her cheeks and her face was drawn with worry and confusion.

"What?" said Zarah in surprise. "But you've got to do it! We all agreed."

"It's ... complicated," Rose mumbled.

Just as Rose spoke, Jessie's eyes landed on one particular photo. It was of three people, all hugging, all smiling. Rose – or at least a smaller, younger version of Rose – was in the middle, with a big beaming smile Jessie didn't know she had. Something clicked in Jessie's mind and she suddenly understood why things felt complicated for her friend.

"What a lovely photo," she said, and turned to smile brightly at Rose. Jessie saw her gulp, then smile back.

"Thank you," she said softly. "It's my favourite."

Zarah and Shanice were looking at each other, confused. They knew something was going on but weren't sure what.

"Can I show them?" Jessie asked.

Rose nodded.

Jessie lifted the photo from the shelf and walked over to the other three girls.

"That's me," said Rose, pointing to herself. "And that's Mum Kim." Now she was pointing to the tall woman they'd seen downstairs.

"Who's that?" asked Shanice, pointing to the woman on the other side of Rose. The woman was hugging Rose just as tight as her Mum Kim was.

"Wait a minute – she's the waitress who was offering us carrot cake just now, isn't she?" said Zarah.

"Um, yes," said Rose. "But she's a bit more

than a waitress."

There was a long pause while everyone looked at Rose.

"Go on ..." Jessie said, not wanting Rose to feel awkward any more. As soon as she'd seen the photo, Jessie had guessed that maybe Rose worried some people might be funny about *her* particular family.

Rose took a deep breath. "That's my Mum Shelley."

"You have TWO mums?" Shanice said.

Zarah's mouth hung open, like a pretty but pretty *surprised* goldfish.

"So, do both your mums drive you crazy, or is it just your Mum Kim?" Jessie asked with a big grin. She wanted to talk normally about Rose's family, cos it *was* normal.

The OMG Blog

Just a different kind of normal to some people's.

"*Both* of them drive me nuts!" said Rose. "It's not just the fact that they live like this or want me to be arty and musical like them. It's just that they're both really confident and think I should be too. They think I should be proud to tell the world 'I've got two mums!' But it's not that easy."

"Because some people are idiots?" said Shanice.

Rose laughed, but Jessie realised that this wasn't always so funny for her.

"Yes, cos some people are idiots," she agreed. "I've been so nervous, starting at a new school, and wondering what people will think. It was OK at primary school. All my friends and their parents knew and were totally fine with it.

Anyway, it wasn't till I got older that I realised some people might find it hard to get their heads around."

"Well, *we're* your friends now, and we're totally fine with it," said Zarah. "So don't think you're getting out of blogging!"

Rose laughed again, and as the four friends came together in a big group hug, Rufus bounded over and joined in with an excited bark and a lick. His tail wagged so wildly it knocked Rose's music stand and sent her sheet music flying onto the floor.

But neat-freak Rose didn't rush to tidy it.

Jessie smiled, loving the fact that Rose was too relaxed and happy to care.

OMG! ♡ ♡ ♡ ♡ ♡ ♡ ♡

Welcome to *Our Mums – Grrrr!* The blog where we tell our mothers we love THEM, but not the mad, bad and sad stuff they do!

→ ## THE YOU-DON'T-REALLY-GET-ME MUMS ←

Posted by Petal

Guess how much I love you?

To the moon and back!

That was our favourite bedtime book when I was little.

And even if I'm all grown-up now, I know you both still love me to the moon and back (and maybe just a little bit more).

But loving me isn't everything.

I need you to *understand* me too.

And sometimes I think neither of you get me at all, which is pretty funny (but not *funny ha ha*) since YOU'RE always saying that people have the right to be themselves.

Well, I'd like to be this version of me, please.

I'm not shiny and amazing and confident like you are. I don't love living in the busy, cluttered way you do. It makes me feel like I can't breathe sometimes. Also, I'm kind of shy and private. I think that's OK, and I wish you did too.

Please get used to the idea that I won't be an artist or a chef or a classical musician – all the sort of stuff that you'd like me to be. Actually, what *I* want to be is a dentist, but I haven't told you that because I think it'll freak you out!

Hope you'll understand.

I love you both (to the moon and back), but grrrrrrr!!

Petal

$\longrightarrow$

Posted Friday 23rd September

CHAPTER 9

SLAP
BANG

The OMG! posters were done.

All six of them for all six of the school notice boards. And each one was customised in a way that meant no one could miss them – hula style!

The girls had sat at the kitchen table at Rose's the previous day and wondered what wild themes they could come up with using glitter, glue and random craftiness. Then Jessie had noticed the pile of crinkly tissue paper that Rufus had sent flying with his tail.

The coloured paper reminded her of Hawaiian flower garlands. And so each OMG! poster had a bonkers border of layered, fluttering flowers.

"More, please!" ordered Zarah.

One of her hands was holding a poster on

the notice board. She held the other hand out, waiting for Jessie to pass her drawing pins.

"There," said Jessie, dropping four pins in her palm. (She noticed little glints on Zarah's headscarf. Glitter from Rose's sparkly – but messy – flat.)

Zarah had put their blog poster up right beside the one about rugby. Jessie almost felt sorry for the boys whose blog it was. No one would pay any attention to their dull poster now. It was like putting a parakeet next to a sparrow, or a rainbow next to a rain cloud.

"That looks AWESOME," said Shanice. "Hey, everyone – check this out!"

Some older students stopped, wondering what was going on. Rose shuffled out of the way, so they could get a better look.

"Hey, that's pretty cool," said one girl, coming closer.

"What's it about?" asked a boy in the group.

"It's a new blog that you can check out this weekend," said Zarah.

"Don't forget to 'like' it. AND leave comments. And tell your friends ... and you can write your own posts too!" said Shanice, acting like an over-excited puppy.

"Come on," said Jessie, grabbing Shanice by the elbow. "Let them read it for themselves. And, anyway, the bell is about to go."

"Aw!" said Shanice, who was enjoying herself showing off the OMG! blog.

Still, she let herself be pulled away and the four girls walked off together. Soon they'd go their different ways, to their different lessons.

But they still had a few more minutes to chat about their chances in the competition.

"I'm going to message my sister Clare and give her the link to the OMG! blog," said Jessie, pulling her phone out of her pocket. "She'll leave a comment on my post, for sure."

"Hey, and we can all ask our Form Teachers if we can tell our class about OMG! at registration time today," said Zarah. "Think about it – that's, er ... four times twenty-eight people. Which is ... err?"

"One hundred and twelve," Jessie and Shanice said together.

"And with that lot and then everyone else in the school looking at our posters today, that'll hopefully mean lots of views for OMG!" Rose added.

"Yeah, at break and lunchtime I'm going to grab people and drag them over to the posters!" said Shanice. "That way I'll make sure as many –"

"Look!" Rose interrupted. "Someone's looking at the poster on the gym notice board."

She was pointing down the corridor, where a woman in jeans was standing, smiling.

"It's a teacher," said Zarah. "But which one? Anyone know her?"

Jessie looked up from the message she was sending her sister.

She smiled at the idea of teachers checking out OMG! And why not? They had mothers, too. And maybe their mothers drove them crazy as well. But, just as fast, her smile slipped away. She was in danger of running slap-bang into someone she really didn't want to.

"It's not a teacher," Jessie mumbled. "It's my mum."

It was as if Jessie's mum sensed her close by ... at that exact second, she turned away from the notice board and began walking directly towards the four girls.

"Hey, Jess-kin!" she called out and gave her a wave.

"Uh-oh," muttered Jessie, wishing she could somehow escape. Perhaps the ground could open up and swallow her. She'd settle for a passing space-ship swooping down to abduct her right now.

The thing was, Mum had been standing reading the OMG! poster. What if she looked in Jessie's eyes and could somehow just tell it was her project? Her idea, even?

Jessie knew all too well how amazing mums

were at knowing stuff about their kids, like when they were sad or worried or upset or hiding stuff. (Pity they weren't so good at knowing when they were driving their daughters crazy!)

"Hi, Mum," Jessie replied in her best don't-bother-me-now voice. She could hardly go barging past her mother, much as she'd like to.

"Oops!" said Mum, clocking Jessie's annoyance as she came closer. "Sorry – I'm not supposed to call you 'Jess-kin' in public, am I, darling?"

And I don't want you calling me darling *either*, Jessie said to herself.

Behind her someone was sniggering. It was Shanice, for sure.

"So," Mum carried on, "are you going to introduce me to your friends?"

Jessie didn't dare make eye contact with any of the girls. This was all too awkward and strange.

"Uh ... this is Zarah, Rose and Shanice," she said in a rush.

She heard them all say wary hellos.

"Lovely to meet you," said Mum. "Now I don't mean to be pushy –"

Pushy! Jessie remembered the title of her OMG! blog-post and she blushed.

"– but can any of your parents help out with teas and coffees on Monday evening?"

There was a moment's silence. None of Jessie's friends had a clue what her mum was on about. Mainly cos Jessie had completely forgotten to give out the flyers that Mum had given her.

"Oh, er ... here," said Jessie, quickly pulling

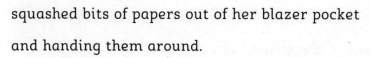

squashed bits of papers out of her blazer pocket
and handing them around.

"Jess-kin!" Mum said with a dramatic sigh.
"You didn't give them out! And I'm really, *really*
stuck for helpers at the meeting."

"My mum will do it, I'm sure," Zarah offered.

"Mine too," said Rose. "I'll ask them, anyway."

"Yeah, and my mum will probably be up for
it," Shanice joined in.

"Oh, thank you. What lovely friends you've
got, Jess-kin!" Mum exclaimed.

*I don't think you'd say that if you knew what
we'd done*, Jessie thought.

"Actually, would all you girls mind giving me
a hand at the Welcome Evening too?" Mum asked,
out of the blue. "I'll need help setting out chairs
and tables and things."

Jessie shot a quick look at her friends.

Their eyes were wide with guilt.

But Jessie's mum thought they were looks of excitement.

"Well, do you fancy it, girls?" she asked with a hopeful smile.

There wasn't much Zarah, Rose and Shanice could do but nod and say yes.

"Super!" said Mum, clapping her hands together. "Well, the Head Teacher will be there to meet and greet all the new Year 7 parents, so I'll make sure and tell him what fabulous Year 7 helpers we have ..."

BRINNNNGGGGGG!!

The start-of-day bell jangled, making them all jump – but setting the girls free.

"We'd better dash, Mum," said Jessie.

"Of course. And I'd better check we have everything we need for Monday evening," Mum said, turning to head off to the store room.

Jessie was just about to hurry away with her friends when Mum said one last thing.

"Oh, by the way, Jess-kin – I mean, Jessie – have you seen that hula-style poster back there? The one with all the flowers on it?"

"Er, nope," Jessie lied. This was awful! Trickles of sweat were breaking out on her forehead.

"I didn't get a chance to read it properly, but it's about some blogging competition," said Mum. "You should check it out, darling. Maybe you and your friends can enter it?"

"Maybe," said Jessie, and then she broke into a run.

Behind her she heard the patter of her friends' feet running too.

And full-on bursts of laughter.

Clare
last seen today at 19:15

OMG – your OMG! blog is so cool! You and your friends are so smart to come up with it. I'd NEVER have the imagination to dream up something like that. Go, go, go, little sis! Win that competition! Love&stuff, C x

19:02

CHAPTER 10

a bit
Second-Best

Jessie was in a bubble of happiness.

It wasn't *just* because she was spending Saturday with Dad.

It was because of the message Clare had sent her last night. In the message, Clare had said Jessie that had a great imagination, much better than hers. That compliment gave Jessie *such* a buzz.

Yes, she'd had good ideas this week. From big stuff like the theme of the blog to small stuff like the crazy, eye-catching posters.

Being with her new friends, doing this project ... they'd both helped Jessie realise that maybe her new school would be OK. She didn't need to feel she was in the shadow of her perfect sister. Maybe Jessie wasn't a straight-As student like Clare, but she was beginning to see that she might just have her *own* talents. She could stand in her own spotlight.

And the best thing was, the OMG! blog was coming to life. All their ideas were working.

Students were looking at it, liking it, commenting on it and posting on it, too!

Since she'd been with Dad all day, Jessie hadn't checked it out for herself. But Zarah and Rose had texted earlier, telling her how popular the blog was getting. And, just that second, Shanice had texted to say the same.

GO US! GO US! Seen the blog stats today???? Who's going to win this competition? We are! OMG! OMG! OMG! S xoxoxo

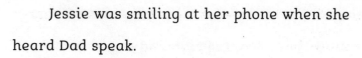

Jessie was smiling at her phone when she heard Dad speak.

"Everything OK?" he asked.

It was Dad's gentle way of reminding her that it wasn't great to be looking at a screen when you were supposed to be talking to someone.

"Oh, sorry – just one of my new friends saying hi," she told him, and she slid the phone into the back pocket of her denim skirt.

Jessie and Dad were sitting at the table in the living room, while Tanya dashed back and forward from the kitchen bringing endless dishes of food through.

"Thanks, Jessie," Dad said, then changed the subject. "Anyway, it's a bit strange having one empty place, isn't it?"

"Yes," said Jessie, realising that he too was thinking of her sister, so far away at university.

There were four chairs at the round table, but only three people would be having dinner together this Saturday evening.

"There!" said Tanya, sitting down at last. "All your favourites, Jessie. Get stuck in."

Jessie winced.

It *was* all her favourite food. The table was piled high with macaroni cheese, sausages, broccoli, coleslaw, potato salad, cherry tomatoes and garlic bread. But it was a bit of an odd mix and she wished Tanya hadn't served all of them at once.

And she wished, too, that Tanya wasn't watching her like that, expecting her to eat lots of it.

After all, Dad had taken Jessie to the cinema that afternoon and spoiled her with hot dogs, popcorn and ice cream.

Tanya knew that, but she'd *still* cooked stupid amounts of food. It was kind of her, but there was something about the kindness that made Jessie squirm. It was like a display, as if she wanted to prove to Jessie what a great step-mum she was.

Whenever Clare and Jessie stayed over, they'd end up giggling about Tanya and her strange meals when they were in the bedroom they shared at Dad's. Of course, there'd be no Clare to giggle with tonight ...

"Oops! Let's get these out of the way so you and I can see each other better, Jessie," said Tanya.

She reached for the vase of pale pink roses in the middle of the table and moved them over a little.

Jessie hadn't even noticed the flowers, or the fact that they were in the way. She'd been too busy chatting to Dad while Tanya was pottering about.

"They are *so* pretty, aren't they?" Tanya commented. "Your daddy gave them to me, the silly, romantic fool."

Jessie bit her lip. This was typical Tanya, the part that really made Jessie squirm. Why was she always trying to show how much Dad loved her? Why did she need to be loved more than his first wife?

Tanya seemed to forget that Dad's first wife was Jessie and Clare's mum.

"Mmm," muttered Jessie. "They're nice."

She couldn't wait till bedtime, when she'd get the chance to go to her room with Dad's iPad. Then she could write a post about how much her step-mum made her go grrrrr ...

"So, how's your week been, Jellybean?" asked Tanya.

"*No!*" Jessie screamed inside. Lately, Tanya had started using Dad's nickname for her, and Jessie couldn't stand it.

"It's been OK," she replied with a shrug and stuffed a big forkful of food in her mouth in the hope that Tanya wouldn't expect her to say any more.

"Jessie was telling me that school is getting better," Dad answered for her. "She says she's met some nice girls in her year."

"Oh, I'm so pleased for you," said Tanya. "It can't have been much fun lately. Not having anyone to hang out with. Apart from your mother, of course. Is she still doing lots at the school? She's always there, isn't she?"

Great. Now it sounded as if Tanya was having a dig at Mum. Tanya made a point of coming along with Dad to school concerts and stuff, but she'd never offered to help out, the way Mum did. Maybe she thought she was too good for it.

And yes, it drove Jessie mad to have her mum popping up around every corner at school, but she wasn't about to say so to her step-mother.

"I suppose Mum is there a lot just now," Jessie replied. "She's getting things ready for the Welcome Evening on Monday."

"Sorry, Jessie," Dad apologised. "I can't make

that meeting. Like I told you earlier, I'm away for work next week."

"That's OK, Dad," said Jessie. "I understand."

"Still," Dad added cheerfully, "I'm sure the Head Teacher will say *exactly* the same things he said at Clare's Welcome Evening, so I won't miss much."

Dad was only fooling around, but what he'd just said made Jessie feel a tiny bit like his second-best daughter. She felt a sudden stab of hurt. And a sudden stab of understanding. *Sometimes*, she wondered, *does Tanya feel like she's Dad's second-best wife ...?*

"Well, *I* can go!" Tanya announced.

Jessie nearly choked on a cherry tomato.

"Oh, of course," said Dad. "If you really want to."

"If I really want to?" Tanya replied, sounding almost snappy. "Darling, I think you'll find the term *Parents' Evening* covers parents, carers, guardians and *step*-parents. Isn't that right, Jessie?"

"Uh, yes. I guess so," said Jessie.

"You know, her mother is always so busy at these events," said Dad, "it'll be really useful if you're there to hear all the school news."

"Isn't that great!" Tanya gushed, patting Jessie's hand. "While your mum is serving tea and biccies, I'll be there for you."

Jessie found she had a new talent.

Smiling while trying to stop her head from exploding.

Grrrrrr!!

Just wait until bedtime and her chance to blog …

OMG! ♡ ♡ ♡ ♡ ♡ ♡ ♡
Welcome to *Our Mums – Grrrr!* The blog where
we tell our mothers we love THEM, but not the mad, bad and sad stuff they do!

→ ## THE WICKED STEP-MOTHER ←

Posted by Jellybean

OK, I'm joking ... my step-mother is not wicked.

She is nice.

She spends ages cooking all my favourite things to eat when I stay with her and my dad. She takes me and my sister on shopping trips and buys us stuff. She's always chatty and friendly and nice.

So what's the problem?

Well, all that niceness feels so FAKE!

It's as if she does all this stuff to impress us.

As if she's trying to prove that she is SO nice that

we can't blame Dad for falling for her once he and Mum had divorced.

As if she's trying to make me like her more than my own mother.

Well, sorry, but it's not going to happen.

I'm not taken in by all the fake nice-ness. It doesn't ring true for me.

Cos when me and my sister aren't there, I bet my step-mum's SO pleased. Really pleased, not fake pleased. I bet she loves having Dad all to herself without his two daughters getting in the way.

So, technically, my step-mother is not a mum. I like her. But she still deserves a grrrrrr!!

Jellybean

→

Posted Saturday 24th September

CHAPTER 11

little Miss
MESS-UP
Strikes Again

It felt so strange being the only student in the school hall. In the *whole* of the school, in fact.

"Here – plug this in for me, please, Jess-kin," said Mum, and she handed Jessie a long black lead and flex.

Mum's words echoed in the vast, empty room. It wouldn't stay empty for long, of course.

It was Monday, 6.30 p.m., and nearly time for the Welcome Evening. In twenty minutes, the hall would be full of students and their parents.

Or, as Tanya pointed out during tea on Saturday, parents, carers, guardians *and* step-parents ...

Jessie gulped when she remembered that. When Dad had dropped her home yesterday, he'd told Mum about having to miss the meeting cos of work.

Mum hadn't been too impressed with that.

Then Dad told Mum about Tanya coming instead of him.

Mum was even *less* impressed by that piece of news.

"Sure, Mum," said Jessie. She bent down to plug in the lead for the big silver tea urn.

Above her, Mum was busy setting out plastic cups and boxes of teabags.

"The Site Manager is on his way with a trolley full of folding chairs," Mum chattered. "And then when your friends get here, you can set them out in rows, please."

Standing up again, Jessie glanced out of the window and saw three bikes sailing across the playground. Two were pretty standard, but one was white with garlands of fake flowers wrapped around the handlebars.

"That's Rose and her parents arriving now," she told her mum.

But Mum was already saying hello and shaking hands with someone else.

"I'm Mrs Bashir. Call me Hana. Zarah said you needed helpers?"

Jessie turned to see Zarah with her mum. Mrs Bashir was wearing the most beautiful purple beaded headscarf. Jessie noticed that she had her phone slipped into the side of her scarf.

"Well, thank you very much! I'm Sandra and this is my daughter, Jessie," said Mum. "Come on around and I'll show you where everything is."

As Mrs Bashir joined Mum, Jessie escaped to

Zarah's side of the table.

"It's kind of freaky having our mums meet up, isn't it?" whispered Zarah.

"Tell me about it!" said Jessie.

The two girls stood hunched and awkward for a moment – but were saved by the Site Manager. Before he'd even parked his rumbling trolley, Jessie and Zarah ran over and began yanking the folding chairs off it and began setting them up.

"Hi!" said Rose, joining them as they were half way along the second row.

Jessie and Zarah were pleased to see her, but even more freaked out to see her mums meet theirs.

"So, you guys brought cake," said Jessie, watching as Mum greeted Rose's parents and

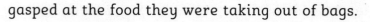

gasped at the food they were taking out of bags.

"Mum Shelley made extra at the café today," said Rose, biting her lip.

Jessie wondered if the others were thinking what *she* was thinking. That the more chummy the mums looked, the more guilty she felt about the OMG! blog.

"Here's Shanice," said Zarah, before Jessie could ask her how she felt.

Shanice saw the girls at the same time, and bolted away from her mother's side, leaving Joy stranded at the tea and coffee stand.

Luckily, Joy wasn't the shy sort – how could she be in that orange and pink shift dress and yellow skyscraper heels? – and she was soon happily introducing herself to Jessie's mum and the others.

"You know who I just saw?" said Shanice, with wide eyes. "Miss Singh! That could be bad, right?"

Jessie was confused. Why did Shanice seem so concerned? At the Welcome Evening, the Head Teacher and some members of staff would give talks. The choir and the school orchestra would sing and play a few songs. It was all meant to make the parents feel pleased that they'd sent their kids to Newton Academy.

So maybe Miss Singh would be doing a little speech about the ICT department.

So what?

Jessie wasn't the only one who was confused.

"But why does it matter if she's here?" asked Zarah. "Isn't it good? None of us saw Miss Singh at school today. If we catch her *now*, we can ask when the winners of the blog competition will be announced."

"*I* get it," said Rose, suddenly paler-than-pale. "Our mums are here, right? So what if Miss Singh talks about our blog on stage and points us out?"

"Don't worry – I wouldn't do that to you," said a familiar voice.

The girls stopped clattering open the folding chairs and stared at their ICT teacher. She'd overheard what Rose had just said.

"Look, girls, I know you created that blog as a private place where students can sound off about their parents," Miss Singh said with a smile. "I'm not going to blow your cover! I'm only here because the Head Teacher wants me to talk about the new computers the ICT department are getting this year."

All four girls breathed a sigh of sheer relief.

Yes, it was bizarre to see their mums all together, chatting and getting to know each other. But at least they didn't have to worry about being found out.

"Now that people are starting to arrive," said Miss Singh, "can I give you a hand getting these chairs arranged?"

The next few minutes were a blur of clanging and banging as the rows took shape. No sooner had the girls and Miss Singh set out one row, than it was filled with parents and students.

Music plink-plonked in the background as they worked. A Year 11 girl was playing some tunes on the piano to entertain the people drifting in.

Finally, the last row was done and Jessie,

Zarah, Rose and Shanice leaned against the back wall, exhausted.

The room was crammed with students and parents, either in their seats or huddled around the table where the girls' mums were serving drinks and homemade cake.

"What do you think's happening over there?" Shanice asked.

She frowned over in the direction of the cake and drinks table and the crowd buzzing around it.

Lots of people were laughing. Some were even dancing.

"Shall we go see?" said Jessie.

She pushed herself off the wall and wandered over, followed by the other girls. Now people weren't just laughing and dancing – they were whooping!

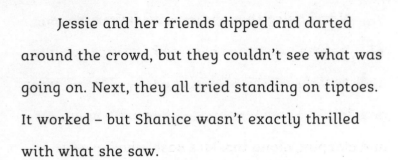

Jessie and her friends dipped and darted around the crowd, but they couldn't see what was going on. Next, they all tried standing on tiptoes. It worked – but Shanice wasn't exactly thrilled with what she saw.

"Nooo!" she groaned.

Jessie's heart sank for her friend.

Everyone was staring at Joy, who was acting as if the serving area was her personal stage. She was singing and dancing along to ABBA's 'Dancing Queen', the tune the Year 11 girl was now playing on the piano.

"Oh, she is *so* embarrassing!" Shanice moaned, thunking her head onto Jessie's shoulders.

But as Shanice tried to make the sight and sound of her mother vanish, Jessie realised something.

No one else thought Joy was embarrassing.

It wasn't just the cheering huddle of parents and students on *this* side of the table. Jessie's mum and Rose's mums Kim and Shelley were singing and clapping along too. Mrs Bashir had even slid her phone out of her headscarf and was filming Joy's moves, her hand shaking as she laughed and tapped her feet in time to the rhythm.

They were loving her. She had transformed the dull and ordinary meeting into something lively and, well, extraordinary.

"Actually, your mum can really sing," said Jessie.

"I suppose so," said Shanice, daring to look up. "She tried out for *The X Factor* when I was little, before Ty was born. She got through to the second round of auditions."

Admitting that, and noticing how warmly people were reacting to her mother, Shanice stopped hiding her face. She started to look more pleased and proud than embarrassed.

"Wow!" gasped Rose.

"Did she really?" said Zarah. "Did anyone in your family record it? I'd love to see that!"

"I dunno … I'll have to ask," said Shanice. Seeing how impressed her friends were made her relax a little more. She even started smiling. "Y'know, I guess my mum's OK, really."

"Joy's more than OK – she's amazing!" said Jessie.

But at that moment, she noticed her own mum's smile slip away. Jessie frowned, wondering what was wrong.

And then she saw.

Tanya had arrived. But she wasn't just sitting in the audience – she was coming to say hello to Mum, and to hand her a plastic tub of cupcakes.

Jessie saw Mum manage a weak smile. She took the cupcakes and said a clipped "thank you".

Tanya turned to go, but Rose's Mum Kim, thinking she was another volunteer, waved her to come and help.

Tanya's face lit up at being included with the other mums, and she instantly got stuck in and began to arrange cakes and serve teas. Mum looked about as pleased as if she'd heard that Jessie had got Detention. And lied to her about it, more than once. (Er ...)

"Ladies and gentlemen, parents and carers, boys and girls ... can you take your seats, please?"

It was the booming voice of the Head Teacher, Mr Frazer. It was louder than ever thanks to the microphone on the stage.

Jessie and her friends slipped away, back to their spot against the wall.

Mr Frazer's voice was loud, but it was also flat and dull, and as he talked, Jessie's mind wandered.

She gazed over at the tea and coffee table. The mums were serving the last few customers, and chatting while they tidied up the empty cups and plates, sweeping up cake crumbs and wiping down spilled tea.

Mum and Tanya were at opposite ends of the table, both smiling, both busy, but both with an uncomfortable edge to them.

Jessie bit her nails as she watched their body

language. It was only when Zarah nudged her – hard – that she realised she should be watching something else.

The big white screen behind Mr Frazer, for example.

The big white screen with the OMG! blog flashed up on it.

"What!" Jessie murmured in shock.

"And while we're talking about how well the Year 7s are settling in, I'd like to show you this," Mr Frazer boomed. "I was chatting with one of our ICT teachers earlier today, and she was telling me about the fantastic response her department has had to a competition they set up."

"Miss Singh said she wouldn't let this happen," Rose whispered frantically.

"Look at her," Shanice hissed, pointing to a shell-shocked Miss Singh, sitting bolt upright at the side of the hall. "I don't think she knew Mr Frazer was going to say this stuff."

"The Year 7 students had to work in groups, and develop a unique blog-site of their own," Mr Frazer carried on. "Here's one of the most popular ones." He had a clicker in his hand, which he pointed at the screen, and one by one the first few blog-posts scrolled up.

Jessie's, Zarah's, Rose's and Shanice's.

All with their nicknames on, but all with nicknames – and moans – that their mums would recognise pretty quickly as belonging to them.

"Oops!" said Mr Frazer. "I hadn't realised what this blog was about. Sorry – hope none of our mothers in the audience spot themselves. Ha!"

Mr Frazer clicked again and moved onto the blog about rugby.

"I think it's OK," said Rose. "He scrolled really fast, so they might not have read it properly."

Jessie hoped she was right. She glanced over at the refreshments table to see what their mothers had made of it all. And what she saw was Rose's mums and Joy frowning up at the screen. But Mrs Bashir was tapping on her phone.

"Oh, no ... my mum's searching for the OMG! blog, I bet," Zarah muttered.

And then it wasn't just Mrs Bashir staring at her mobile. Jessie's mum and Joy were gazing down at it too.

Jessie heart sank.

She was Little Miss Mess-Up all over again.

Cos it was *her* fault that Mum would be sad and mad at her.

Worse still, it was *her* fault that ALL the mums would be sad and mad with their daughters.

If Jessie hadn't suggested the OMG! idea at lunch last Tuesday, Zarah or Rose or Shanice might have come up with something much better, much safer. Maybe a blog about how horrible homework is. Or which YouTube clips are the cutest – kittens in unicorn hats or babies dancing to 'Uptown Funk' or something.

Anything apart from a blog where you moan – in *public*, for the whole world to see – about your mothers ...

Jessie suddenly felt like the least perfect, least brave, most dumb kid ever. And there was just one imperfect, cowardly, totally dumb thing

she could do.

And so she ran ...

Clare
Online

Hey sis – I have goofed up SO badly. You said my blog idea was really imaginative. More like a really imaginative way to cause a complete DISASTER. Mum just found out. In front of the whole school! If I had any money I'd jump on the first train and come hide in your student room for ever. (At the moment I'm hiding in the girls' toilets at school. Yuck.) J x

19:14 ✓✓

CHAPTER 12

Locked in Shame

Jessie had run past the nearest girls' loos and headed instead for the ones at the far end of the corridor. She reckoned she'd be harder to find there.

And so there she sat marooned on the lid of a loo seat, resting her burning forehead against the cool wall of the cubicle. She might as well stay locked in here for ever, locked in shame.

Cos how could she face Mum after what she'd done?

Then there was Tanya ...

Jessie suddenly broke out in a cold sweat. Until that moment, she hadn't even considered what Tanya would think about the 'wicked step-mother' blog-post.

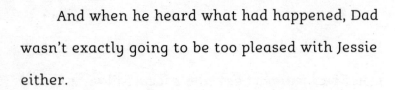

And when he heard what had happened, Dad wasn't exactly going to be too pleased with Jessie either.

Help ...

Jessie clutched her phone, willing her smart sister to get back to her with some words of wisdom.

But when a WhatsApp beeped in, it wasn't Clare.

Rose
Online

Where are u, Jessie? Things are OK. My mums have been great. They've said sorry that I felt that way and will do better at 'getting me'. They're not mad. I'm sure your mum will be cool too! Rx

19:19

Nice as it was, her friend's message didn't help one bit. When Jessie closed her eyes, all she could picture was her mum's face, full of hurt and disappointment. And she couldn't picture a cosy Saturday tea around the table at Dad and Tanya's anytime soon ...

CREEEEAKK!

The sound of the main door to the loos opening made her jump.

"Jessie? Is that you in there?"

Zarah had tracked her down.

"Yes," Jessie mumbled.

"Do you want to come out?" asked Zarah.

"No," said Jessie. "I never want to come out."

"Oh, don't say that, Jessie! Please open up," Zarah's kind voice pleaded from the other side of the door.

"No. How can I? I feel terrible," Jessie snuffled, wiping tears and snot away with the back of her hand. "The stupid blog was my idea. I've caused all sorts of hassle for everyone."

"Actually, I don't think that's true," replied Zarah. "I just talked to my mama. She was a bit cross at first, but she said sorry, she didn't know she'd been embarrassing me with her over-friendly comments. She's promised to stop doing it – if I promise not to let Maryam dye my hair red again. So I think we'll be all right."

"What about Shanice?"

"Oh, Joy just laughed about it. You know how she is. Nothing fazes her. And Rose's mums were fine with –"

"I know," Jessie interrupted Zarah. "She sent me a message. But I don't think it's going to be that easy for me to sort out. My mum is going to be SO angry."

"No, I'm not, Jessie."

Jessie froze. That was her mum's voice. Had she come in at the same time as Zarah?

"Mum? How did you guess I was here?" she asked in a small, shy voice.

"I didn't guess – you got in touch with Clare, and Clare got in touch with me," Mum explained. "Zarah just showed us where the loos were."

Jessie's heart lurched. Mum had said 'us'. That meant she wasn't alone ...

"Hello, Jellybean," came Tanya's voice.

Jessie stared in shock at the back of the cubicle door.

"Jess-kin," Mum carried on. "Listen, I think the last few years have been difficult for all of

us. And if I've been pushy with you and Clare ...
well, it's only because I love you and want you
two to do well for yourselves. To be brilliant and
independent. That's all."

Of course Mum felt like that.

Of course Jessie suddenly understood.

Of course her now-single mum wanted her
daughters to be independent. She didn't want
Jessie and Clare to have to rely on anyone,
especially a man, for their future happiness.

Of course Mum's voice wobbled a little as
she talked.

Of course Jessie badly wanted to run out
and hug her – but she was too worried about
facing her step-mother. "And the thing is," she
heard Tanya say, "you girls *are* brilliant and
independent. I've been quite *scared* all this time."

Jessie blinked her teary eyes.

"Scared?" she said softly.

"Yes, scared of your mum, because she's so strong and capable, and a bit scared of you and Clare too."

"Of us?" Jessie repeated, confused.

"I'm scared that you don't like me," came Tanya's reply. "Not really."

So that's why Tanya was always so full-on. It explained the over-the-top gifts, the endless giant meals, the chit-chat that sometimes seemed silly and annoying. Tanya wasn't fake. She was just scared – and a bit daunted.

"I'm sorry ..." mumbled Jessie.

"Oh, don't be, darling," said Mum.

"No, don't be," Tanya joined in. "It's like your friend Zarah said. What's happened is all right. More than all right, really. We should be thanking you girls – you've reminded us how important it is to be honest. And it's given us all a chance to hear each other. Even your mum and me. Who knows," she added, and Jessie could hear the smile in her voice, "maybe us mums will get together and start our own blog about you girls …"

As Jessie thought about what Tanya just said, she saw something slide under the door. Two somethings.

Two phones – one Mum's and one Tanya's.

On Mum's screen were the words *I LOVE YOU*.

On Tanya's – *ME TOO*.

Jessie hiccupped – half a giggle, half a sob. But before she got up and opened the lock, she sent one quick text to Mum and Tanya …

☺

OMG!

Fans of OMG! — exciting news!
It's been given a face-lift.

Welcome now to
OH MY GOOF!

the blog that lets you spill your
most embarrassing stories.

Done something **DORKY**?

Said something beyond **STUPID**?

Caused a **TOTAL DISASTER** when you
were only trying to help?

We've all been there, done that,
and usually survived.

So come on — let's all share the
shame and smile about it!

Site created by Jellybean, ZeeBee, Petal and IceGirl

Have fun
and stay safe online

The internet is a wonderful place to explore, discover and share information, connect and communicate with others and be creative. Here are our top ten tips for staying safe and happy when you're online.

1. Don't give anyone online personal information they could use to find you in real life or to contact you in other ways, such as your address, school details, email address or mobile number.

2. Remember that any photos or videos you post of yourself can be seen or downloaded by lots of people. Think carefully about what you are happy sharing. Imagine you were going to hand the picture to a queue of strangers on the street instead. Would you be happy for them to see it?

3. The same is true of what you say. Some people behave differently online and offline. They may say rude or hurtful things online they would never say to a person's face. Think carefully about what you post and respect other people as you would in the offline world.

4. Keep your privacy settings as high as you can.

5. Don't befriend people you don't know and remember that not everyone online is who they say they are.

6. Don't meet up with people you've only ever met online. If someone suggests meeting you, tell your parents or another adult you trust.

7. If you see something online that makes you feel scared, unsafe or worried, leave the website and tell an adult you trust straight away.

8. If you are being bullied online, tell an adult you trust what is happening so they can help you deal with it.

9. Keep a note of any messages or texts, take screenshots and don't delete anything. This will help you explain what is happening.

10. Don't respond to bullies and block any accounts sending you anything that upsets you. If the abuse is happening on a website or social media site, report it to the site.

If you are at all worried about your safety online and need to talk, then you can call this free helpline for children and young people. The counsellors at ChildLine won't judge you and will help you work out what you can do. They offer comfort, advice and protection.

ChildLine (UK): 0800 1111
www.childline.org.uk

Karen McCombie

When she was little, Karen McCombie dreamed of being a ballet dancer or a window dresser making displays in shop windows. But instead she started work as a fashion editor, quiz-creator and pet correspondent for lots of different teen magazines. These jobs taught her the very useful skill of writing quickly and clearly and she is now the bestselling author of over 80 novels.

Karen's favourite place to write is a small room in her house that looks out over her garden – and her second favourite place is a café just round the corner, which feels like home but has the added advantage of selling big slices of cake. However, Karen says that if she was given the choice between a slice of cake and a bag of crisps she would choose ... the crisps every time. In fact, the sound Karen likes best in the world is the noise of a bag of Ready Salted being opened.

When she was growing up, Karen lived in Aberdeen where she could see the North Sea and its oil rigs from her high-up window on the 15th floor of a block of flats. That was quite a long time ago and Karen now lives in London with the loud, funny, Scottish person who she's married to, the lovely, funny, cute person who's her daughter and a beautiful daft cat called Dizzy. But she still likes gazing out of the window, watching the clouds and thinking up ideas for her next book.

You can visit Karen at www.karenmccombie.com